A Lobster Tale

BY BIG TOM & HENRY LINDLEY

And in the end

The Love

you make

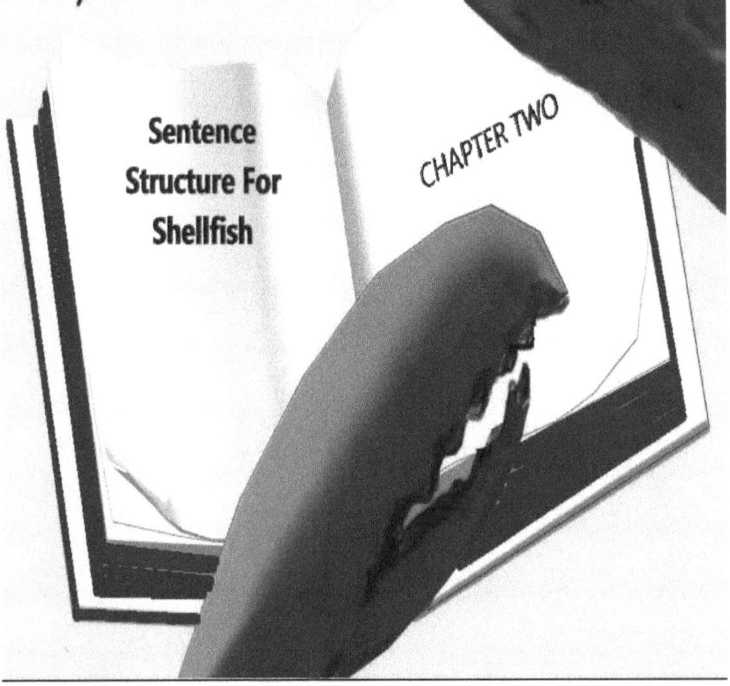

Sentence Structure For Shellfish

CHAPTER TWO

A LOBSTER TALE

By

Henry Lindley

TABLE OF CONTENTS

DEDICATION

This work is dedicated to my sister I. Taylor and Brother, J. Lindley as well as my cousins Ann and Casey, brothers from other mothers Mr. M. Bell, Mark J. Miller, my missing friend Scott Brown. As well as the many who inspired me with their encouragement and the lending their names to some of the characters. And in loving memory of the Ginger.

A LOBSTER'S TALE
BY HENRY LINDLEY

The town of Big Bay was anything but big; in fact, it wasn't really a town so much as a village. Just a small grid of narrow streets that divided a few cottages and modest homes from the "commercial" center, a few seasonal businesses and the year round, widely-renowned restaurants that crowded the longest and widest street. This street ended at the docks and, because it was so near the seafood served in the restaurants, could, and often did, boast that it had the freshest in the world.

These bistros were so highly regarded that their patrons drove in from the cities nearly every night crowding the small streets and thronging the restaurants. Many among these multitudes considered Alberto's to be the best of the best and many thought themselves to be very lucky to get a table.

Alberto's specialty was "Mediterranean style seafood" though it bore little in common with the cuisine for which it was named. Still, it was quite good, and the business had sustained the Salvadoet family for five generations, each son taking over for his father and not just the duties of manager but actually adopting the character, if you will, of "Papa Antonio". This would include the formal dress and the feigned, broken English accent. This affectation would never fail to make his daughter's eyes roll. His friends, and those in the know, called him Alberto.

The current Alberto was just in his late twenties and a Johnson & Wales graduate. He had back-packed all over Europe after his junior year in college and, after what can best be described as a misunderstanding, but more accurately characterized as a strong-armed robbery at a youth hostel in the former Balkans. This young Alberto resolved to make a go of the family business and in turn make his father, mother and, no doubt the elder Alberto happy in whatever situation or location they were to find themselves.

The current incarnation of Alberto adopted the formal style of the latter Alberto, black tie and tails and, most importantly of all, the tried and true menu. Many a wide-eyed intern from some highly touted culinary institute would approach Alberto every year with an idea to update the menu. Alberto would take them aside and laying on his thickest and most fatherly accent, he would admonish these novices saying, "no broken," pausing for dramatic effect and then continuing with the final word on the subject, "no fix."

CHAPTER TWO

Captain Scott was a force of nature. He was the captain, commander and absolute ruler of the "Penny Pincher." Penny, as she was commonly known, was the most "ship-shape" of all the vessels in the bay, and this is likely from where the term came.

Most of the younger captains and many of the crewmembers had learned their skills under the steely, aquamarine gaze of the tall, broad shouldered Captain Scott. Of course they would never call him anything but "captain" to his face as a sign of respect. But Captain Scott also knew how to have fun, and it was because he was that rare man that understood the need for both discipline and diversion that his crews, past and present, loved him. He also mystified them because those piecing eyes seemed to see beyond just the rolling of the sea and the ever-changing sky. Captain Scott seemed to take it all in: the sea, the sky, the seafloor and the movement of all the creatures in their environments. That is not to say that he never misplaced a pot or failed to get his limit. This was the business of fishing, after all, and Captain Scott had a wily adversary in the local lobster population. But it was this sixth sense that he sometimes possessed that would take Captain Scott to waters other captains had considered worthless or played out. It was many a tourist, observing from the dock, but within earshot of the other captains that Captain Scott, "must be part lobster himself, because he surely thinks like one". And though these casual commentators were often embarrassed having made these comments out-loud, they weren't far from the truth.

Captain Scott considered that if any captain were to make the claim of understanding this particular prey, he would place in the top three. The old timers, those that were long beyond crewing and of such an advanced age that they felt secure in making the claim would comment directly to Captain Scott telling him he was good, but would never be as good as (they would fill in this blank with some "old salt" they had crewed with, or were fond of).

Captain Scott would always, nod his head, smile and agree with them. He would never be the sailor that, "such and such" was, or had been. This was part of the respect that Captain Scott paid those that came before him and he assumed would be paid to him in the times to come.

But that was the future, and the task at hand for Captain Scott was the lobster season. Given his noted talent, drive and desire for success, the actual meeting and subsequent relationship that developed between the famed Captain and what must have appeared to him, at first, to be a large, even bloated lobster, with an unattractively bent antenna was perhaps inauspicious. But meeting Big Tom was a seminal event.

Brought to the wheelhouse by an unorthodox crewmember, Captain Scott's twelve-year old, precocious daughter, Penny, who held the prodigious Big Tom out for inspection. As Captain Scott examined Big Tom from stem to stern, as it were, Big Tom regarded Captain Scott in much the same manner.

"What have you found there Penny?"

Penny regarded her father whom she loved very much but felt that she knew him better than he thought. "He isn't for lunch!" Penny twisted her finger through her pigtail, an endearing habit her father noticed because he did have a better understanding of his daughter than she thought.

"No, not lunch, though he'd be a meal for the whole crew." Captain Scott smiled at Penny. "So who is our new mate here?"

Penny knit her brow for a second and then said, "Larry. I think I'll call him Larry."

Captain Scott regarded Big Tom and really looked at him the way people do when they seem to have seen something different in something they have seen a million times before.

Something in those piecing eyes of Captain Scott saw the glint of being, more than just a mammoth example of a lobster; there was something different about this creature. Captain Scott couldn't put his finger on it but there was something very different about this specimen. "Well, aren't you a big fella then?" Captain Scott addressed Big Tom. Big Tom in turn waved his antenna around in an effort to communicate, "Could you put me in some water please?"

"Bet you'd like to get wet, huh?" Captain Scott said. He waved to a crewman and a bucket was soon sitting to the side.

Big Tom's size could scarcely fit in the bucket and his antenna stuck out like radio towers, though one was bent to the side. Captain Scott placed the bucket on top of the galley hatch allowing Big Tom's antenna to survey anything they might. As it turned out this was a very happy accident for Captain Scott, Big Tom and the entire crew. While Captain Scott had been attending to Big Tom's quarters, such as they were, the Penny Pincher, underway as she was, had drifted very close to the edge of the channel.

Big Tom knowing these waters as well as you might know your own neighborhood, tapped Captain Scott on the arm. When Captain Scott glanced down at Big Tom, Big Tom tipped his bent antenna toward the channel marker piling.

"That-a-way, you think?"

Captain Scott quickly spun the wheel and the Penny Pincher chugged out to deeper water. Captain Scott glanced down at Big Tom and said, "Good call." He paused a moment not sure just what to call his newly acquired crustacean perhaps navigator, or maybe crewmember. Larry seemed to be too familiar for what was, after all a workplace environment. But in the end he opted for the term "mate." It was fitting and respectful and given the newness of this relationship, all and all, proper.

This seemed to please Big Tom and he flipped his antenna in the manner of a salute. Captain Tom rewarded him with another chunk of bait, which also pleased Big Tom, and he tore into it with relish. Penny nodded knowingly and turned to go, saying as she reached the hatch, "And I thought he was going to be <u>my</u> pet."

This mutually beneficial relationship between Big Tom and Captain Scott may have gone on nearly indefinitely. Captain Scott was a man in the prime of his life and, assuming no misadventure, a lobster can live for decade upon decade. However it was Alberto that spied the "look-out lobster" in the wheel house of Captain Scott's boat and began a campaign to relocate Big Tom, or "Larry" as they came to call him, at Penny's insistence, to a tank at Alberto's restaurant.

Alberto pointed out that Captain Scott was by far the biggest producer with his well-known sixth sense and even with the help of Big Tom the catch was little more than "humble pie." This was after-all, the business, and a hard scrabble business at that, and the facts of life of commercial fishing, fish or lobster are caught and consumed. Whereas, Alberto reasoned, heatedly, if he is said to have ever done anything heatedly, it might be said that placing Big Tom in a suitable, highly visible location in his establishment would increase demand and thereby, literally, profit both the men's businesses.

That was logic that was difficult for Captain Scott to argue with, and, though he would never miss an opportunity to slip by and see his old crewmember, he finally relented, and Big Tom was moved to his special quarters.

It was understood and agreed by both men that "Larry" would never really be listed on the menu and his presence would provide something Alberto called "marquee value". And in fact he did become something of a local celebrity. He was often stalked by a particularly large omnivore that could have easily made a meal of him. But, true to his agreement, Alberto would always intercede and offer this patron another tempting morsel. This left Big Tom, more or less, to his own observations of the comings and goings of the clientele.

It was from just this spot, his quarters, and his idle time as mentioned that he first saw the young couple as they entered.

CHAPTER THREE

The young couple entered Alberto's timidly but at the same time lost in their own world of happiness. Big Tom sensed this happiness and noticed that many of the other patrons also sensed this otherworldliness, as the happiness appeared to percolate through the room.

Big Tom would learn that the couple had just come from the church where they had said their vows. This couple was Oscar and Susan. And Big Tom would also learn that Oscar, the groom and a broad shouldered man with dark eyes, was an engineer. It was a bit harder for Big Tom to understand what it was that Susan did, but it was something to do with managing wet lands.

Big Tom was amused by the idea of wet land. To him wet land didn't make any sense. You had either land, which was wet when it rained, but was mostly dry and then there was everything else. And to Big Tom everything else was home.

Big Tom thought about home, and he thought about those of his kind that disappeared from the tanks and were forgotten. Here it is hard for us to understand, but Big Tom knew that this happened everywhere, even more so at home, and so he focused more on his happy situation and what he might learn. Big Tom thought a lot about how important it was to learn everything he could. And Susan took a singular interest in Big Tom. Their shared passion for learning brought Big Tom and Susan closer than most.

In the coming years she would never fail to speak with Big Tom and advise Alberto on his care. Everyone in the restaurant was drawn to Susan. She had an oval face framed with dark blond hair and large blue eyes that shone with kindness and understanding. She moved with an athletic grace.

But that first day the biggest thing Susan did was save Big Tom from her new husband. "No," she had said. "He is a magnificent creature! Imagine what he could tell us." Big Tom had never thought of himself as a magnificent anything, but he liked the sound of it and his antenna swept back and forth like radar.

Oscar nodded and patted Susan's hand. "I will never be so selfish about shellfish again." Oscar looked down at Big Tom, "My apologies to you sir; may you have a long and happy life."

Alberto appeared at Oscar's elbow and directed the couple to a nearby table. They did not see the flip of Big Tom's antenna, a sign of affection. As the couple crossed the room following Alberto a murmur of whispers raced through the patrons and an immediate presumption was made that this young couple were the "outsiders" come to fill the vacancies at the college.

Jimmy Alderman, the former director from the local college, had retired to some mountain community having had his fill of developers and small town political intrigue. Some were sorry to see him go, and others, not so much.

It is like that in small towns, large towns, big cities and even countries, but everyone involved had come to the conclusion that "new blood" was just what was needed.

It was remarked, much later, that had Oscar arrived on his own, and been identified as the new administrator, he may have found himself at the center of a loud "discussion" complete with finger pointing and accusations. But the couple would find themselves well liked in the community. Because of the amiable attractive young couple even old adversaries suddenly were willing to reconsider formerly stubborn positions.

Alberto delivered menus and bread and filled the water glasses. "Welcome to Alberto's and pleasant we make your meal." Oscar and Susan nodded as Alberto marched away with his usual precision.

"I have something for you", Susan said.

Oscar replied, "You have already given me more than I could have hoped for."

"Nevertheless," said Susan, and she withdrew a small wrapped box from her purse and placed it in front of Oscar.

"But my dear," protested Oscar. Susan nodded and Oscar carefully un-wrapped the box. Oscar pulled an old pocket watch from the box and held it up. "It's beautiful", said Oscar, "like a work of art. But I have my…"

"Phone, yes I know, but there is something more to this" said Susan. "And I want you to know it comes from the heart."

Oscar popped open the watch face and read the inscription on the back. The inscription read, "Our love is timeless, Susan & Oscar". Oscar clutched the watch to his heart and said, "I will never let this go!" Oscar took Susan's hand in his and kissed it.

After Oscar's declaration he and Susan noticed that the whole room was silent and listening in on their private conversation. When they glanced around the room they could see that the patrons were smiling, really beaming back at them. Then, realizing that they had been listening in on a private conversation, the patrons suddenly began to busy themselves with their own conversations and own affairs.

From where Big Tom sat he could not see what was inscribed on the watch, but he knew that something special had passed between these two people. It was at that moment that Big Tom became a believer in true love and destiny.

OUR LOVE
IS TIMELESS FROM
SUSAN
11 12 1
10 2
9 3

CHAPTER FOUR

Not far in terms of distance, but in almost every way, in another world, under the sea there was a small clutch of lobsters born. Among this group would be a female lobster that would grow up to be called Little Bit.

Little Bit was not especially smaller than any average lobster; it was a playful nickname given to her by her father. He was proud of his daughter's strength and independence, though that independence would sometimes cause them to clash. He had often said that she was a little bit of heaven with just a little bit of the other place. Little Bit, the very descriptive name stuck. She will become much more important to our story a little later, but it is significant that we mention her now because if it is true, that opposites do attract, then that can truly be said of Big Tom and Little Bit.

While Big Tom was a quiet and introspective creature, Little Bit was vivacious and lit up any situation in which she found herself. No doubt being the center of attention at Alberto's had made Big Tom less impressed by the spotlight.

Later, when they would meet, this predicament would put Little Bit in the position of making the first move to engage Big Tom. Life and love present us with such problems and we just have to make the best of it. Little Bit certainly would make the best of it and, though she was frightened for perhaps the first time in her life, she was to find that Big Tom was nothing like she had imagined. Things are often not what they seem. Big Tom seemed and was large, but he was friendly and thoughtful. Little Bit saw that there was more to him than just his size. It must also be noted here that much of a male lobster's early life is unknown to this day. At some point in their young lives they depart their home waters for an extended sojourn, the whereabouts a mystery. Many, of course, never return and their fate is less mysterious. They are all compelled to take to the open sea in a sort of vision quest where their experiences will alter the course of their lives. This journey makes them who and what they are. Big Tom never spoke much about his experiences. Still, rumors persisted about mass stampedes across the sea floor with no apparent destination or obvious purpose. There were fights of course, terrible and, again without obvious provocation, just part of being a male lobster. Big Tom bore the scars of these fights, though he never spoke of them. It is likely that his size caused him to be drawn into more of these fights, his bent antenna an unwanted souvenir from a spirited bout, no doubt.

Wherever his travels had taken him, though, he had the wisdom that travel will bring. Big Tom was not quick to judgement and believed more in what was done than what was said.

As for Big Tom's thoughts about Little Bit, he saw her strength and admired her ease in any situation. It can be said that he was as glad to meet her as she was to meet him.

CHAPTER FIVE

From Big Tom's vantagepoint at Alberto's, he could see the comings and goings of all the customers and wait staff. Many of the customers would nod or even speak to their local celebrity. Among these regulars who would speak were Oscar and Susan. These visits were especially enjoyable to Big Tom. Susan never failed to inquire about Big Tom's health and well-being, even going so far as to insist that the staff and Alberto himself insure Big Tom's general happiness. Sometimes she would pass along a tasty morsel, provided by Captain Scott, whom she got to know well. Big Tom would savor these treats, but they would sometimes remind him of the ocean and his times with Captain Scott.

Oscar would often join his wife in addressing Big Tom, though less animated than Susan. Big Tom felt that they were truly happy and had never lost that feeling he had sensed when they came in that first day. Oscar would nearly always ask, "So they are treating him right, are they?" And Susan would nod and respond, "He is thriving physically."

This note of something not mentioned, not considered, when she spoke. What did she mean? What was she not saying? Big Tom would ponder this in his slumbering hours. He would also remember that Oscar was always wearing his big, shiny pocket watch.

The watch was a source of some teasing that Oscar would receive from the other regulars that he and Susan had come to know over the years. They would stop by Susan and Oscar's table and point to the watch telling Oscar he should "get with the times." They would hold the latest device that doubled, or quadrupled as a watch, a phone, or a food processor, shaking it disapprovingly at Oscar. Big Tom noticed that Oscar would beam at Susan and pat the watch in his pocket. Oscar would just nod to these folks and say they were right, but he continued to wear the watch.

CHAPTER SIX

As is often the way of people this pattern continued. Oscar and Susan and the various cast of regulars came and went. Big Tom slumbered away and saw these comings and goings and nothing seemed to change. But nothing is sure in this world except change. Some change is like the "second" hand on Oscar's old watch; we can see it moving and can see the change right before our eyes. Then there is the "minute" hand of that watch that is moving but moving so slowly that we can't see it. In fact, these hands seem to be standing still. If we look away for a few moments and then back at the hand it is obvious that it has moved forward, and time has marched on.

Such is the confounding nature of time that mankind has devoted no small effort in an attempt to measure and somehow control this unseen but undeniable fact of our lives. We've built monuments to it, and the technology developed and devoted to its measure has risen to the level of art. And still it crawls, or zips by unnoticed. We get up in the morning and go to work or school, and though we have good days and bad days we find that it is almost impossible to live in the moment and be aware of the life, our life, that is passing by. It even seems wasteful, when thinking about the passing of time, that we take these moments to consider that time is passing. These moments of reflection, perhaps even those that are happening right now, are the very things that allow us to understand that time is passing and the recrimination that we have wasted some of ours. It is this predicament that spurs us on to try to "live in the moment" even as we are reflecting upon the moments passed and in effect not living in the moment of that reflection. So we might say that thinking about thinking, and thinking about thinking about time are worthwhile pursuits, as long as they are not all we do. Or do too long!

After all, a diet of only cookies and cake is as unbalanced as that exclusively of bean sprouts and kale. Big Tom understood that his life was not balanced at the moment, but he had faith that, as surely as Oscar's watch counted off the seconds, minutes and hours of the day, an unknown adventure would come his way one-day. These were the thoughts that bubbled through Big Tom's mind. He knew there was more to life, his life, all life, than his quarters at Alberto's and the liveliness he observed there.

CHAPTER SEVEN

It's surprising, given all the thought Big Tom had directed at the consideration of time, that he really didn't take note of its inevitable passing. He would notice the absence of this or that regular now and then and of course the ever-changing wait-staff, but, like the minute hand of Oscar's watch, these were slow changes slipping by inconspicuously.

Big Tom's concern was raised one day when he spotted Susan and Oscar arriving. Susan stumbled near the doorway and though Oscar was able to arrest her fall, Oscar had to assist Susan as he brought her over to visit with Big Tom.

Big Tom could see the same spark of life in Susan's eyes and her warm smile that had always made him feel good. But there was something else in Susan's eyes. She seemed to be looking toward some distant horizon that neither Big Tom, or even Oscar, for that matter, could see. Big Tom's antenna swept the familiar contour of her face and though he detected the subtle wrinkles that appeared around her eyes when she laughed, he had not taken these as signs of age. He simply saw her as his friend. Susan and her wonderful laugh were as enchanting and delightful, as he had ever known.

Big Tom had noticed a change in Oscar's demeanor. He seemed more pensive and a bit nervous, and though he had always been attentive to Susan, he now beheld her with a more soft and loving gaze. There was something different in Oscar's eyes as well. Something that Big Tom could not quite define. It wasn't exactly sadness, though it was a bit sad, it was more helplessness and feeling of loss, but Big Tom could not understand.

Shortly after the stumble Big Tom began to notice the changes that time had brought to his little world of Alberto's. Though Susan and Oscar still made their visits, fewer and fewer of the old group would turn up. Big Tom even observed that Alberto's wildly untamed hair was growing thinner and grayer. Alberto still moved with practiced precision, but he was a half step slower.

If Big Tom could have seen beyond this little world of Alberto's, out into the village of Big Bay, it is doubtful that he would have recognized anything beyond the docks and the ocean. Big Bay had become a sprawling jumble of vacation condos, cottages and gaudy mansions built to impress the casual observer rather than to serve as retreats for the rarely visiting owners. Perhaps it was best that these sights were beyond Big Tom's horizon.

As we have said before the only certainty is change, and Big Bay had changed. Whether that change was for the good or bad is for us to decide for ourselves. But it is sure that some change was for the better, and some would surely be considered for the worse. But this is the nature of change.

CHAPTER EIGHT

When Big Tom began to see these changes in his long-time friends he naturally had mixed feelings. He was glad to still have them and recall the best of times they had shared, but he was disturbed by the appearance of their best clothes that were worn, faded and shabbier than he had recalled. Alberto's meals were still robust and filled the platters to the edge, but they seemed less opulent. The regulars did seem to savor the edibles and never failed to compliment Alberto and the staff. The wine, extravagant desserts and other extras were reduced in portion size, but still available, though consumed less vigorously. The patrons still appeared to relish these treats with a nostalgic fervor.

Though Big Tom never suffered any diminished feeding or attention, he was mindful of something different in the atmosphere. Whatever it was, it wasn't clear to him, but it led him to another thought: that being the fact of his disengaged, almost aloof, position of observer. He wondered why he seemed to have been chosen to witness the events playing out before him and yet not be able to influence them in any way. Big Tom felt himself no different than Susan and Oscar, other than the obvious fact of being a different species and confined to a tank. This state of being, this idea of being with "them," even a part of "them," and yet not one of them lit a fire in Big Tom's mind that he would wrestle with for the rest of his life. What was it, who was he, and what did it mean?

CHAPTER NINE

We find ourselves underwater with Little Bit sitting opposite of Big Tom. "Well, what did it mean?" she asks. She is asking about the story of his life on land, which suggests that it was some time in the past. In fact it was in the not too distant past and we shall see how Big Tom came to be back "home," though that is far from the end of his story.

"There is no easy answer for that, Little Bit. But I did learn some things, and some things we never can know, or ever decide that we know."

"That sounds confusing," said Little Bit as she rubbed one claw against the other.

Big Tom stroked her antenna with his bent antenna. "Yes, confusing and amusing as well", said Big Tom.

"Are you making fun of me?" said Little Bit as she raised herself up on her haunches.

"No," said Big Tom. "But you do make me laugh…" Little Bit's claws opened into attack mode. "But you make me laugh because you make me happy. There has never been a dearer, or sweeter," Big Tom paused searching for the right word. "Friend" he said at last. "Is that the word?"

Little Bit settled back down into a relaxed posture and folded her claws. "Friend is OK, I guess."

Big Tom laid his antenna on Little Bit's claws. "You know you are really so much more than that. Please forgive my awkward speech."

If Little Bit could have smiled, lobster anatomy being what it is, she would have. She did have a warm feeling in her thorax and her eyes were gazing into Big Tom's. She looked away and said, "You're not too bad yourself. But I wish you would explain this to me a little more."

"I'll try, but it might just be more confusing," said Big Tom. "Things in life are mostly unclear, at least until we have the advantage of time and distance to consider them." Little Bit scuttled closer. "It might be fun," she cooed.

Big Tom rested his head on his big claw. "I can only speak for myself. My life, even from the beginning, hasn't been typical, maybe not unique, but definitely different. At first I just scrambled to stay alive like anyone. I was lucky and grew quickly. I mean the luck came in the fact that my size kept some predators away. Of course, it also made me a target for some others that were more ambitious. But thinking back on it now I have decided that I was lucky and survived, and survived in spite of the fact that I had something in me that drove me beyond the path that others took. I was determined to see the world. I saw a lot of things, did a lot of things that I can never tell you about but the drive was strong in me and brought me back here. Though it may take me on to some further unseen destiny, I was compelled to come back to the home waters. It was that same drive that made me climb into the trap".

Little Bit's antenna went up, "You knew better. What were you thinking?"

"I knew better, but I knew that the trap was a gateway to another world."

"Weren't you frightened?" Little Bit exclaimed.

"Yes, and foolish to take such a risk. But I was drawn to see, to know. I was young, and, like I said, very foolish." Big Tom rubbed his claws together. "The strangest thing happened though. I found a whole new world filled with strange creatures, but having spent time among them I came to understand that they were not so different as you and I." Big Tom rubbed his claws together. "I couldn't let anyone else go, or anyone else's word for it. I had to see for myself."

Big Tom remembered the day he climbed into the lobster pot. He scuttles over to a large pot where a few smaller lobsters are struggling to free themselves. Big Tom yanks the wire mesh open and frees all the smaller lobsters. He waves the smaller lobster away and admonishing them to not be so foolish in the future, he climbs into the wrecked pot and settles down to wait.

CHAPTER TEN

While Big Tom was on the job at Alberto's, the other players in our story, indeed the whole wide world, were playing out the dramas, disappointments and euphoria of their own lives. Anyone lucky enough to live a long and observant life, will see fashion come and go; collective wisdom, if it can be said to be a type of wisdom, will also come and go and in many cases, come again in some haggard disguise. Big Tom could, and did see these machinations come and go and made no judgement. These attempts at camouflage were quite well understood as some manifestation of a courtship ritual. The idea of his own experienced courtship ritual would usually sweep these musings regarding the customer garb of the Alberto patrons from his mind and send him into a mild depression and an uneasy feeling, not perhaps fear, but a definite uneasiness.

Big Tom was often to over hear the phrase "There is nothing new under the sun." And he understood the sentiment and could understand the merit of this observation from the patrons of Alberto's, but because of his long and protracted life-span he could see that the "new" they sometimes prized was not in fact new, just a fresh turn on an old idea. The patrons believing that their thought or action was "new" and unique, was a variant on something Big Tom had seen what seemed like a millennia ago. But Big Tom was anything but judgmental. He would come to understand after many years of contemplation that man was a creature who lived more in the moment. He knew man was capable of reflection and consideration in matters that ran from dissuading themselves from touching a hot stove to thinking about the happiness and needs of others. In this way, almost a back door, Big Tom didn't realize that he had discovered his heart and that it was open to a phenomena humans had thousands of words for, though Big Tom was only now comfortable with the term "affection".

Affection implied more than just passing interest, but also allowed for some distance. Big Tom had great affection for Little Bit, but a big lobster needs a lot of convincing to commit to the three words that he was afraid to utter to her. There would be time he thought, surely there would always be time. Some later, distant future that would be more suitable, more perfect. But Big Tom would not know that he didn't have as much time as he thought. He would come to understand that no creature would have enough time.

CHAPTER ELEVEN

Big Tom gave a lot of thought to what was happening "topside" as he had heard Captain Scott call it. Big Tom knew what was likely going on aboard the Penny Pincher. He could imagine that second mate Bradley, the third son of a legendary lobster dynasty, who was not interested in lobster fishing at all but had a keen interest in industrial farming. Bradley would pass those few moments of down time on the boat by thumbing through his well-worn copy of "Modern Farmer Magazine." And though Captain Scott and the rest of the crew would tease him, they also admired him for having a dream of his own. Bradley was saving his money, and one season he never reported for duty. Sometime later Captain posted a picture of Bradley covered in dirt and standing beside a broken down tractor. Bradley's grin was so infectious that the whole crew had to smile and wish him well.

Big Tom had spent so much time with Captain Scott that these memories came easily and he thought of them nearly every day. However he realized that although he had spent a much greater time with Alberto he observed that he knew very little about him. Indeed the lives and renderings of those prior Alberto's, so lovingly displayed, only added to the enigma.

Alberto rarely spoke to Big Tom, and it was never more than pleasant small talk, and Big Tom paid no heed to the gossip of the wait-staff, many of whom were just passing through, perhaps only a season, the sleepy village of Big Bay. This group had to manufacture their own drama to pass the time. Big Tom dismissed this idle chattering out of claw, but being a "local" or, more properly, "live-in stock", he had a unique vantage point in which to view Alberto up close and in his unguarded moments.

Big Tom recalled many a night where Alberto, his shirtsleeves rolled up, sat hunched over a table with large ledgers and stacks of invoices piled around him. On more than one occasion Big Tom had seen smears of ink on Alberto's brow and an accompanying look of worry in his usually kind eyes. Sometime in the small hours of the morning Big Tom would hear the sound of approaching footsteps and presently Maria, Alberto's wife would appear. She would drag Alberto away from his ledgers saying, "The figures can wait and a rested pair of eyes might find a solution in them." Alberto would smile at Maria and nod. It was obvious that in Alberto's eyes there was one and only one Maria and after many years of marriage he still put great stock in her opinion and advice.

Alberto often recalled the day that they met and the day he fell for her. He had been rushing around what was his father's Alberto's restaurant, his arms filled with dishes. She had been seated with her aunt and she noticed that his shoe was untied. "Let me get that for you", she said.

"Oh no, miss I'll –," but before he could stop her she had tied his shoe, and, smiling up at him, said, "We can't have you dropping the company profits, can we?" Then she laughed.

Alberto had never heard such a laugh. He was smitten. He glanced over to the bar and saw that his father and mother were watching him. He only saw them for a second, not long enough to see his mother squeeze his father's arm, but they somehow knew what he was about to discover.

Alberto smiled at Maria and thanked her. He even offered her and her aunt, of course, a free entrée. Big Tom noted that sometimes the smallest of incidents could lead to the biggest of changes. And no matter how late Alberto was to fret over these documents, the next morning his shirt would be crisply laundered and his tie, no doubt straightened by the loving hand of Maria, would be clipped and in place.

With his trademark smile, Alberto would be as cheerful as a man without a care in the world.

CHAPTER TWELVE

While Alberto put on a brave face to the world, Captain Scott wore the same expression most of the time. They said he was inscrutable, and this was so, but it wasn't by his design. Captain Scott was a man who thought ahead, and the truth is that he was thinking most of the time. He gave no consideration to what expression was on his face and thought even less, if that was possible, about what people might be thinking about that expression and whatever it might betray about his thoughts. But even Captain Scott's thoughts were more muddled than usual. He couldn't concentrate on reading the sea or the signs that had always led him to the big catches. For just as Alberto fretted over the business books of the restaurant, Captain Scott had to worry about the cost and uncertainty of the fishing industry. The catches had been dwindling for the last few years and though Captain Scott, his crew, and the rest of the fleet adhered to a set of strict regulations about the size and number of the catch, the same could not always be said of large commercial enterprises that swept by Big Bay from time to time. These interlopers and their nets scooping up any and all life indiscriminately.

Captain Scott and the other captains that plied their trade in these waters did so with care and a kind of reverence. They respected the ocean and the bounty it could provide.

It was that bounty upon which Alberto, and indeed the town, depended. So it is no wonder that these lives that were so intertwined were to develop a sense of trust and dependence that isn't often found outside the confines of small towns, no matter where they might be located. But in one such as ours, so closely tied to the sea, friendships ran deep, and trust, though earned, was not a rare commodity.

Given this state of affairs it wasn't a huge leap of faith for Alberto to listen and agree to Captain Scott's plan.

CHAPTER THIRTEEN

It must also be noted that those admiral traits of trust and community were not limited to the land dwelling inhabitants of this little corner of the world, for even that expression "little corner" is more than insignificant and misleading. It can truly be said that every part of the world is connected to every other part, often in strange and unexpected ways. But that part of our story will come later, for now let us consider only a small part of the vast community that inhabits the coastal waters just offshore.

Let's consider Big Tom's kith and kin, the lobsters. Though it would be a mistake to assume that "they" are just like "us." Remember that even all of "us" are not alike in thought, or mood or outlook. It is this idea of outlook that "they' must be very different from "us." Their sense of time, given the extraordinary length of their lives, must be very different from ours. Of course we are just assuming that given this treasure of time they may indulge in deep and ponderous thought. Perhaps they plumb the depth of the meaning of life, all life, all over the world, or the universe, for all we know. They had the time and certainly the depth, in a manner of speaking.

What might the purpose of life be? Or perhaps some of them, perhaps most of them, are merely thinking about what, or who, or where they might be having, or being, lunch. So we can assume that they are somewhat like us at least in some regards. Big Tom and his companion,

Little Bit, are certainly like us in their affairs, in so much as they are common concerns: who am I, where am I going, what does it mean, and who and what is important to me in this thing we know as life.

What does it mean to be a friend? These questions and many more were to occur to Big Tom, but not just yet. As it happened he was sitting in a shallow pan of warming water while Captain Scott and Alberto discussed his future.

As you have guessed by now Big Tom wasn't just any old lobster. Besides his size, which alone was enough to get him noticed, and likely eaten, at almost any other time, Big Tom was something more.

Big Tom was also a deep thinker, rare for almost any species, but we can suppose even more rare for an oversized lobster, and as mentioned before he was given to deep thoughts. Not just where did the universe come from and where will it go to, or did time have a beginning and how could it have any end, as well as who am "I" and where do I belong in this realm that seems all too real to my senses.

The deep thought that came to him in this most unlikely hour was a perception that the debate that was going on here just above him, was not unlike a faded, ragged memory that he could not identify as his own, but rather thought it must be a memory of all lobsters, all life in fact. It was a sense of other-worldliness, an echo of the memory from when his ancestors, all our ancestors, scuttled from the depths of the sea and glimpsed the bright light of the sun and the sky and the stars for the first time. The idea that there surely must be more than just what we see. That somewhere, somehow there was something we would call by different names, but allowed that life was something beyond just biology.

CHAPTER FOURTEEN

Big Tom discovered in those few critical moments that he had a particular gift or talent if you will for understanding these truly alien creatures that inhabited a world that was adjacent to his own, but in every true sense of the word, foreign to it. Those creatures he first understood were Alberto and Captain Scott.

Big Tom took Alberto's quiet and outwardly shy manner to belie his true nature, that of drive and ambition. Alberto had grown up in an environment where service was measured in minutes if not seconds and the customer's satisfaction, as capricious as that could be, was the last harbinger of success or failure. Big Tom would later conclude that Alberto's motivation was to quickly find out what you wanted and then, just as quickly, to provide you with what you desired. After many years of observing Alberto, Big Tom felt confident in his assessment of Alberto and truly came to admire his commitment to bringing his customers his very best.

CHAPTER FIFTEEN

Then on the other hand, or claw if you prefer, it's doubtful that Big Tom would have made that distinction, but no matter here, there was the personage of Captain Scott.

Big Tom had much less time to observe Captain Scott, though the Captain was a man with a personality written as large as the sea he traversed; it was in that commonality that Big Tom felt he was able to draw some insight and make some conclusions in regard to Captain Scott.

One factor of which Big Tom was not aware at this moment was that Captain Scott was to save his life. In every true sense Captain Scott saved Big Tom's life in this instance, to boil or not to boil, as that was the question. But in a much larger sense Captain Scott saved Big Tom's life by giving him the time and the literal platform from which to observe and consider and come to understand perhaps as well as any of us who will observe and consider those weighty and perplexing questions that life will present to us.

Captain Scott was no sentimentalist, his livelihood depended on his catching, and his customer ultimately consuming, uncountable tons of those very crustaceans of which Big Tom represented a single, even if an unusually large specimen. In that way Big Tom mattered more to Captain Scott as weight, time to market, wear and tear on the machinery, return on investment if you will allow.

That is not to say that Captain Scott didn't admire the creature. He admired Big Tom in particular, and he held the whole of Big Tom's kind in a type of reverence. These unlikely beasts had been the cornerstone of his families' fortunes for more than a generation. These curious and enigmatic beasts, so oddly formed, and yet so tasty were very much the center of Captain's Scott's thoughts. Though it must be said that some of those higher ideals were less of a consideration than the over riding idea that beat like a bass drum, or more correctly like a Siren's call, in the Captain's head. "This fella is so big people are gonna get hungry just looking at him." When Captain Scott had given voice to this thought it was such an obvious, plain, simple and undeniable truth that even a cautious soul like Alberto had to agree.

Penny
Pincher

CHAPTER SIXTEEN

The plan that Captain Scott had given birth to had been something even more than prophetic. In fact, Big Tom had been such a hit from his very debut, that the fortunes of both men, Captain Scott and Alberto, as well as their subsequent dependants, and even the town as a whole, had risen on that oft mentioned, but rarely seen, "high tide" that so many say "raises all boats", even if few have ever witnessed or benefited from such an occurrence.

Though Big Tom would have surely demurred from any suggestion of he having any part in the town's larger success. In many ways he was the match that lit the fire. And it would not be false modesty keeping Big Tom from any claim of the sum or substance arising from a connection to the town's prosperity, rather a sense that he had begun to feel that, thought joined their pathways, perhaps in a loose, but not random trajectory. He would be pleased that the town prospered, but would feel fortunate to benefit from that happy event, rather than any sort of inciting factor.

Big Tom considered all of the creatures that inhabited the great wide world to be fellow travelers, set upon on a grand journey, the outcome of which was uncertain, but the fact of that ambiguity was the core and binding feature of the voyage.

CAPTURE SEVENTEEN

While Big Tom was pondering these weighty thoughts and the town was experiencing this explosive growth, somewhere, off-shore, not too far away from the growing town, in fact suffering some ill effects from the unrestrained growth, in the coves and inlets that made the location so attractive to the human and the sea-dwelling inhabitants, Big Tom's future mate was growing to maturity.

While as thoughtful and smart as Big Tom, Little Bit was forced to employ her keen wit and eye for danger in what we might refer to as a battle for survival. Humanity, if the reader is of such a persuasion, may have judged many of Little Bit's challenges and her actions in their regard to be cruel. It is in the nature of mankind to judge and to subscribe its indefinite and fluctuating moral code upon any and all other species it considers lesser or not as important. The bewilderment of this fact is that practically no species that shares his dominion can top mankind for cruelty particularly to its own members. This observation aside, mankind has no frame of reference from which to judge Little Bit only in so much as an individual has the right to fight for his or her own survival.

Had Little Bit even been aware of such an arcane philosophic concept she would not have given it any more than a fleeting thought. Her focus and her energies were directed to the very fact of survival. Much later Little Bit would meditate on the contrast of her life's path and that of Big Tom. It was her conclusion, in so much as anything as opinion can be drawn to such, that while Big Tom was a wealth of insight and grasped some of the deeper meanings to life's insistent questions, she on the other claw had what we might term, "street smarts."

Now matter what our terms, the couple would be a formidable pair. Of course these years preceded Little Bit's chance meeting with Big Tom and for his part, Big Tom had no reason to believe that he would ever leave the confines of his accommodations at Alberto's. I can only urge forbearance to the, thus far, persevering readers and assure them that these events shall come to pass in an unlikely and amusing fashion.

Whether it was fate or destiny that would bring the couple together was a question that Big Tom would always side scuttle. "Isn't the fact that we did meet enough?" he would pronounce with a heavy sigh of bubbles.

Little Bit having experienced real danger in her life would tease her "big fella", that not even a mind as Herculean as his could know the thoughts of the ultimate creator. And though he was slow to accept any such belief, as he grew older, he began to understand that everything is not knowable. He resolved to know those things that he could and not blow bubbles at those things that seemed beyond the reach fact or verification.

CHAPTER EIGHTEEN

While Big Tom pondered and Little Bit fought to survive, the village of Big Bay grew into a playground for the rich and famous as well as those of lessor means. "The rain," as the old saying goes, "falls on the rich as well as the poor." And so it could be said by extension that the sun shines equally on those of unequal wherewithal.

Susan and Oscar, once viewed as the "new blood" at best, and "those interlopers" at worst, had become part of the fabric that drew the community together. As time passed and newer arrivals arrived, Susan and Oscar seemed to have always been there. Time, or rather the passage of time seems to share a common trait with light. Light can bend, refract, or recast and certainly distort. All of these peculiarities can be subscribed to time. Any consideration of time, particularly the characteristic of distortion of our memories, is easily understood. The fact that Oscar and Susan had become so much a part of the make up of Big Bay was evidence enough of this phenomenon.

And how different is memory? It is woven into time and like a mirror turned upon itself can misinterpret, twist and fool us all. It is not just the shadow of some event or substance that may, or may not have happened in this or that manner, it may be just a fleeting thought of that substance or event. Some private reflection that was never shared, or perhaps it was shouted from the rooftops of some imagined stage. Time has twisted it, fractured it and often-reinterpreted events, words, or any elements to fit a self-serving narrative. Big Tom was aware of this fact and struggled to understand what misconceptions he could be laboring under.

CHAPTER NINETEEN

Meanwhile the growth of Big Bay plodded forward like the river to the sea. Big Bay saw its share of good times and the ephemeral nature of fame as the celebrated would parade through her streets, only to be replaced by another group of more recently celebrated as the little town became the "it" location. But time and the nature of such fleeting designations would eventually leave Big Bay to the fading memory of those that once held her in high esteem and now couldn't recall just why. The trendy shops and hot-spots would now seem shabby and worn. Such seemed to be the fate of many such locations and Big Bay just took her place in that line of the once, "was" and "now forgotten". It is only cold comfort to know that whatever the next chosen, "it spot" destination would at some point find itself taking a post alongside that of Big Bay.

Big Tom and the town elders had lived long enough to see this cycle and were at peace with it. Big Tom understood better than almost anyone that decay always holds the trump card, shiny and new always gave way to dull, drab and decrepitude. But that did seem to miss the point of living in the moment. So it was quite a shock for Big Tom to see Oscar without Susan.

Big Tom had known that people don't live as long as his kind, well, some of his kind in any event, but still the absence of his friend disturbed him. Later Oscar came and stood by Big Tom's tank and withdrew his pocket watch, the one given to him by Susan on their wedding day and gazed at it forlornly. Speaking to himself, but also to Big Tom he recalled the first day that they came to Alberto's. "You know," he said in Big Tom's direction, "she always wanted to come here to see you and assure herself that you were being treated well." Big Tom had always been treated like a king but in all the hours of his deep concentration he had never considered that someone else would have been so concerned for his welfare. Big Tom raised an antenna out of the water and patted Oscar's sleeve. Oscar smiled and appreciated the gesture. Oscar leaned down as if sharing a secret only Big Tom would understand. "There are so few of us left these days. I know that wherever she is, she has a happy heart to know that you are here and safe." Big Tom felt a warm glow in his hindquarters. A feeling he had never known. It was Oscar that gave Big Tom the words he couldn't find himself. "She loved you, you know. Surely you must have known. In some ways I was just a human substitute for the magnificent creature you are."

Oscar produced a handkerchief from his pocket and polished the shiny watch before wiping a tear from his eye and stepping over to his usual table. Big Tom paid extra attention to the watch and the strange markings that decorated it. With this new sensation growing within him and the kind words that Oscar had shared Big Tom knew without a shadow of a doubt that the markings were something more than commemorative, that whatever they signified they were something more than just their meanings. Somehow these markings held a power beyond the mere words. Big Tom knew that this watch somehow bound Oscar and Susan and in some strange way even himself together in a way in which he could not yet understand.

CHAPTER TWENTY

As the sun drug the earth in its path and the moon drug the tides, the years progressed. There were hard times and there was war, and for all the devices that connected people, people seemed less and less connected. Many of the "fresh faces" that had once sought to fit in and be seen were now the rapidly depleting old guard.

From Big Tom's point of view he saw this and gave a lot of thought to decay and how every ordered thing seemed to drift inexorably to dissolution, disorder and in his word decay. But Big Tom also saw the promise of spring and the hope that seemed to know no bounds. These discords seemed at odds with a world that seemed doomed for ashes. It was under this dark sky of a gathering storm that a summit, of sorts was held at Alberto's. The locals couldn't recall a time when Alberto's had been closed; it had been only on the rarest of occasions, but this was unusual even by Alberto's strict standards.

The locals milled about the front of Alberto's, and some of the bravest even pressed their faces to the glass window to peer inside. Among these was the largest patron that had always greedily eyed Big Tom. It had often seemed his mission in life to devour Big Tom in what he would assume to be an epic meal but would in fact only be a passing pleasure that would be followed by years of regret and accusatory whispers behind his back.

The sight they beheld was as commonplace as corks, or torn fishnets, even short lengths of old hawser, all of which they would behold because these were among the many nautical items that festooned the walls of Alberto's, and almost any seafood motifed restaurant in the wide world.   Captain Scott and Alberto sat at a small table that was adjacent to the tank where Big Tom rested, his antenna visible above the edge of the tank. Captain Scott continually repositioned his cap upon his head. Every few seconds he would lift it up and then replace it in almost the exact same position. You could tell that this was a nervous habit because the bill of the hat wore a clear outline bleached white by the saltwater from the Captain's hands.

Alberto was a man that was used to waiting on people and therefore showed much less outward frustration, but even he folded and unfolded his hands much more than was common. Big Tom's antenna flipped from side to side to match the conversation. "It's clear that something must be done. These hard times can't last forever." Captain Scott fairly chewed the words as he said them and they seemed to have left a very bad taste in his mouth.

"But we have to live through them," responded Alberto.

CAPTURE TWENTY-ONE

It was Alberto's second son, Bob, who first made the suggestion. Bob was quick-witted and dedicated to the family business and also more than a little relived that he was not the first born son and therefore not saddled, as it were, with the moniker "Alberto"; granted it had its privilege, but it also carried some less than desirable attributes such as being the "man out front."

Bob excelled at the behind the scenes peculiarities of the family business. He threw himself into the bookkeeping necessitated by any business and as such had his finger squarely placed on the rise and fall of the enterprise.

Bob was keenly aware that the fortunes of Alberto's were in decline. In his own way Bob was just as quirky as his brother, indeed all of the Alberto's that had preceded his existence, his first love had been geology, and given the adjacent rocky shoreline that was his first playground, this was understandable, but Bob had moved on to physics, which he considered to be a profound attempt to understand the world, but he had come to philosophy when he discovered that there were just some things in the world of Big Bay, surely of the whole wide world, that could never be quantified or labeled. He could never put a number on the sweet salty bite of a new winter's day. Never could codify the beauty that was the wild, untamed ocean that gave his world life and, sad to say, often took it away, randomly, casually and frequently with a perceived cruelty. No scale by which to judge the brightness of the sky or the smile of those townsfolk he encountered daily. Bob did not blame God or nature or the sea for that matter; things just happened thus and so, and he had resolved to accept these as beyond comprehension, if comprehension was even to be considered. What he did find was that in the world of numbers, the ebb and flow of business accounts, there was a certain certainty that not only appealed to him, but in some curious way gave him solace, balance of mind, if you don't mind the use of the phrase in regard to accounting.

Bob was much like Big Tom in his general view of life. What was to be, was to be, but that didn't mean that one was hopeless to change their fate, or the fate of their friends. Time might be a river flowing onward to a sea that we could not observe from our vantage point, but it was just as certain as the sum of two numbers would always be that same sum, unless, as Bob chuckled to himself, there was a modifier, and those modifiers could be just as plentiful and as unseen as those rocks that lingered just under the surface.

Bob knew the limitations of certainty and took great pride in the fact that many certainties were just guesses founded on the shifting sand of assuming that what had generally happened before was most likely to happen again. The argument of conventional wisdom, when it reached his ears always reminded him of the old saying,

"The sound you hear is God laughing at man's plans."

Far from unsettling Bob this opened the door for a confluence of potential futures. His perspective wouldn't allow for him to judge the merit of what would come, but the movement forward was inexorable.

Not unlike Bob, Big Tom felt that he too must serve two masters. The first was the biological drive that most all-living creatures feel and the second was a greater lust for knowledge.

Bob, no doubt, felt the biological urge and would marry a pretty, pale skinned, freckled red head that he met one summer when her family's car broke down while visiting Big Bay during a summer vacation. Bob had ridden his bicycle out to the main road into town and had chanced upon Haley and her well meaning, if not mechanically inclined father. Bob had met his future wife because he had carried his Swiss army-knife and the radiator hose of her father's car had been loose.

Bob would often think about the absurd nature and remarkable randomness of that nature, that was so capable of changing on the smallest, most insignificant of events. The fact that his knife was equipped with a flat-head screw driver, just the tool needed to fix the hose clamp, and the character of the repair, that is the fact that they would have to wait for the hose to cool down, giving the somewhat shy Bob time to speak, and a mutual interest to develop between the future couple.

Between Bob and Haley it was she that would encourage his pursuit of his obvious artistic talent, and she that was largely responsible for the success it would enjoy.

The other keenly felt obligation that Bob held close to his heart was to ensure the success of the family business. Again a succession of events, some small and seemingly insignificant and others titanic and unimaginably irrepressible would impact every aspect of their lives.

Bob would never know that his "bright idea" would be the turning point for Alberto's, Big Tom, Oscar as well as his family and countless others that even we can't see, the ripples on the pond, if you will, stretching beyond our grasp.

If you will forgive this author's note I have often found that we rarely know, or see the impact of our thoughts, be they in print, or not, or our actions witnessed by others. There are many great writers that have illustrated this, "all the world is a stage and mankind are merely actors" to paraphrase the Bard, or, "the pen once written, moves on". I can't claim these as my original ideas but offer it here only as an illustration. We know Bob's intentions were to save his family, his world, but from our vantage point we can see that the ripples, the threads connected and affected events he could never and did never know.

CHAPTER TWENTY-TWO

And so with the idea formed in his mind and seeming to be an inspiration at least, or an epiphany on the order of the discovery of how to make fire at utmost, Bob would pitch his life changing idea, first to his skeptical father and then to the even more reluctant Captain Scott. They would argue with Bob, they would argue with each other, when one would seem to be persuaded to the other's point of view, the one that was the most persuasive would begin to doubt his own reasoning and so the contention ebbed and flowed like the tide that both men were so profoundly familiar with and bound by.

How could they let their "old friend" be put up for auction like some common commodity when he had, in fact, spent most of their lives, and, as far as they knew, most of his life as an important part of their lives.

Bob himself was not as enthusiastic about the idea as he might have been, but he advised the older men that the only permanence that was offered by the world, indeed the universe, was that change was inevitable. While this was of absolutely no, or at best, cold comfort to the two old friends, the fact remained that unless something was done "Larry," Alberto and Captain Scott, in fact the whole enterprise as well as a large proportion of the town, would all find themselves facing changes that were, at best unpleasant and at worse a terminal downward spiral. "The sump-pump in Davie Jones' basement" as Captain Scott colorfully summarized it.

So with this agreement reached, however reluctantly, it would have appeared that "Larry", or rather Big Tom's destiny was sealed. The men had met and though aggrieved, had resolved to do what must be done. Alberto and Captain Scott turned to Bob with the same question. "Well, now what do we do?"

Bob slumped over and spoke in a clear, but measured voice. "I'll arrange everything."

CHAPTER TWENTY THREE

When Bob had uttered the phrase "I'll arrange everything." His motive was to save his father, brother and his father's friend from the minutia of what he assumed would be a stack of paper flyers that he alone would trudge across the small community and persuade the few remaining shop keepers to display what for them was yet another reminder that times seemed to be changing for the worse.

Bob knew that many of these members of the community were in dire straits themselves and had to be wondering if this turn of events was just the first drop of rain in what was looking to be a terrible storm, just lurking a few months, or even perhaps days ahead, for themselves.

All of them knew Bob, all knew Alberto, and Captain Scott was, for all intents, the local spokesman. He had once appeared on a national Sunday morning news program and was questioned by the host as to the sustainability of his industry. The slanted, loaded and unfair questions seemed to predispose that whomever the audience was for this "slice of Americana" it, or they, would be contra to Captain Scott. In the end his segment was cut short and the accepted reason around the town was that he had answered truthfully with an emphasis on good stewardship, responsibility for the natural resource and the balance that all men, and women of course, should bring to their endeavors.

Captain Scott had not been the mean monstrosity the

network had hoped for and therefore was dismissed as an oddity of a dying industry that could amuse the viewers and allow them to feel smug and superior while not considering where their meals were actually coming from.

And you, the perceptive reader, will have realized that these changes had not gone unnoticed by Big Tom. Critically observant, with almost limitless time to consider the ramifications, outcomes, and consequences, he had diagnosed the likelihood that his time at Alberto's would be come to an end. And, like many of his kind, he felt that end would involve boiling water and melted butter.

The leviathan that had menaced "Larry" all these years was still, and the most likely contender, to partake in this most probable ending. There is an old saying about the pen having writ and moving on. However, the improbability of Big Tom's life was not to be so mundane.

CHAPTER TWENTY-FOUR

When Big Tom was a baby, or a "bug" as they were sometimes called by the lobstermen and by the older lobsters themselves, there was no indication that he would grow so large. The old "culls" or those lobsters that had lost a claw would often taunt the younger lobsters. This situation, being short one claw as it were, was not permanent though because lobsters can regenerate claws. You can imagine the "school yard taunts" this fact could, and did, lead to. But Big Tom would listen to the old lobsters and try to find out about the world. Born with an inquiring mind and a natural curiosity, Big Tom would listen to the old fellows, their lives and their adventures. Some of these old guys had learned a thing or two and Big Tom would listen for hours, or at least until they began to repeat themselves.

Some of these old comrades assured Big Tom that the world was made of water and that everything was just a different manifestation of it. The rocks and the sand, even those curious blobs that passed overhead from time to time. But Big Tom dismissed this right out of claw.

Big Tom knew, or just felt that the world would be a much more interesting place and he set his mind on exploring and understanding what the world, the realm where he found himself, was, and just what was his place in it.

This decision, seemingly so natural, so *small, so insignificant, would alter the course of his entire life. He didn't know it then, but there would be moments in his life, in everyone's life, where a small resolution would have such a profound impact and this was his moment. So he left the confines of the small rocky enclave where he was born and headed out into the big muddy world.

His travels would take him all around the world and he was witness to some of the greatest events in maritime history. All this time he would meet other species, those with enough brain capacity to reflect upon their environments and Big Tom would ask them about their histories, their thoughts on the world and just how did they see themselves fitting into this or that situation. Of course many of them saw Big Tom as fitting into their diet, but his size and mobility kept him safe as well as a healthy respect for avoiding phylum that would find him particularly tasty.

He encountered many different modes of thought, but his first supposition must be that the world was real and not just some figment of his imagination. He quickly concluded that though the idea could not be totally ruled out, the fact that he had the idea and was conscience of the world and his thoughts that he and therefore the world must be real. In any event he reasoned that if it were all a dream it was his dream, and he was to follow where his thoughts should lead him. He was well into his sojourn when this idea was settled, and he could have turned back, but he had decided to push on and see where this dream may take him.

As he pondered this idea it occurred to him that the purpose of life was to struggle to live it. There were biological urges thrown into the mix, yet no matter what situation you could find yourself in, your duty was to try and live the best life you could. Now the idea presented itself, just what was "good" and what was "bad" and how could you reason between the two. Clearly there were ideas, thoughts and actions that may benefit you and harm others, but it was equally true of the opposite. Was doing what was best for yourself, better than doing what was best for the group? These thoughts would not be easily dispatched. Big Tom would work out that while there seemed to be a general idea of "good" and an idea of "bad", there were many degrees and shades and conflicts and contradictions among these concepts. And there were those that thought there was no difference or value to any of these conceptions. He was perplexed by the idea that many of these beliefs could be twisted and used to justify any point of view. Big Tom did not arrive at this idea quickly or dismissively.

After pondering these conundrums for many years he concluded, much as he had at the beginning of his quest, that life, his life, anyone's life, be it dream, a nightmare, a phantasmagoria of some greater being in which we are but phantom apparitions playing out some elaborate narrative for their horror, or amusement, we are, nevertheless here to follow whatever destiny we may find.

Big Tom resolved to follow that destiny. His resolution meant that he must explore that part of the world that had been alien and perilous for him. That part of the world that we know as land. It might show our arrogance to think of the world as the land, considering the vastness of the oceans that embody the planet we call home. But this region was an untouched enigma for Big Tom and his life, his mission, was about destiny and exploration. He determined that somehow, someway, whatever he could do, he was bound to learn all he could about these creatures that shared his world but lived such a foreign existence. He knew that all the living entities in the sea knew them and called them, sometimes disgustedly, as "man."

CHAPTER TWENTY FIVE

Big Tom took his time with his return to the waters around Big Bay. He wasn't reluctant to return, nor was he not sure that he had perhaps missed something along the way. He had been an eyewitness to some of the most celebrated and infamous maritime events of his epoch. He had seen the northern lights and the Southern Cross. He had seen and understood the appearance of sea creatures that were unknown to men, the graveyards of many ships, some with their treasure scattered across the seafloor. He had watched the miracle of life and the sadness of death. Those samples of death had often been of a scale and dimension that was nearly impossible to comprehend. Yet he had seen and understood that, although uncharacteristically, his life would be a journey just as he observed with the beginning, a middle and the ultimate end. It was with this thought that he had rounded the horn and crossed the straits with some haste. He did dawdle briefly under the Sargasso Sea. Big Tom loved the drifting mass of life, the plants and animals all floating along on an aimless journey. He didn't judge them by the standards he had set for himself, but he did feel the pull of exploration and thirst for knowledge that seemed to be lost, or forgotten, or at least of no concern to this lazily spinning raft of a communal household.

He diverted once more before the final approach to Big Bay. It wasn't really out of the way and it was a marvel with which Big Tom was enthralled. We know it as the mid-Atlantic ridge, but what so entertained Big Tom was a phenomenon commonly called "pillow" lava. What is happening is that the Atlantic Ocean is expanding, and, as it does, the magma below the surface surges outward. When a ridge of magma cracks open and the hot lava is exposed to the cold sea water, the magma cools quickly into a blob that resembles a pillow like the kind you might find on your bed at home. This act of creation was fascinating to Big Tom and he could watch it for hours. So he allowed himself a bit of time to contemplate this marvel before pushing on to his home-waters.

As he neared the area he was surprised at how little it all had changed. There didn't seem to be nearly as many boats in the water, there was a fair amount of pollution, but Big Tom hadn't known what to expect except perhaps what he found. He scuttled into his old neighborhood and was surprised to be greeted by name from some of the old culls and old-timers that hadn't seemed to have aged a day since he had last seen them. Some even called him by name as if they had seen him only yesterday and he had just returned from some trivial errand.

CHAPTER TWENTY SIX

About the time Big Tom was returning to the area another couple was making their way to the Big Bay region.

This other couple was, of course Oscar and Susan. Susan's work was what had brought them both to Big Bay. If there is such a thing as a typical love story, which your author would argue does not exist, nevertheless, Oscar and Susan had something of a traditional account.

Susan was the smarter of the two and Oscar had adored her from the moment he had met her. He was well regarded in his field; she was the star of hers. Oscar was shy and retiring, a benefit for him, while Susan was vivacious and gregarious. Oscar was so drawn to Susan that although it was nothing within his experience he resolved to take a course in her discipline. As it happened she was the "TA" and taught the lab portion as well.

Call it fate or happenstance, or perhaps a bit of strategy on Oscar's part, but Susan became Oscar's tutor and in this way they really discovered each other.

Oscar discovered that Susan was a scientist and a gentle soul, Susan discovered that Oscar was great with numbers, awkward with people and about the nicest man she had ever met. My readers will know where their story is heading. And despite countless media portrayals of the dominate man, it is the female of the species that generally allows the path to merge, or diverge.

However not known for sure it seems that this same subtlety, or reality plays out with lobster couples as with their human counterparts.

It's hard to say when and where Big Tom caught Little Bit's eye. Little Bit being a feisty female lobster. But once she had laid eyes on him she had set her antenna on the idea of them as a couple and Little Bit was in the habit of getting what she wanted.

In short order Big Tom was arranging the rocks around his hollow at her direction and seemed to be very pleased to be doing so. He told her of his travels and made no secret of his desire to continue his investigation of the land and those creatures known as man. Little Bit was a pragmatic sort, and she knew that lobster life was often the story of those males and even females that ventured out one day never to be seen again. She herself had seen the oddly shaped boxes with the beckoning enticement of free food. She had been warned away from them by countless lobsters, but as a young juvenile she had actually witnessed a friend, on a dare, enter and exit the box with no harm done. But when he had tried to repeat the trick suddenly the box had been jerked upward, and, when the box drifted back to the seafloor moments later, it was absent her friend.

Little Bit had always remembered and was not comfortable with the idea that Big Tom might someday willingly climb aboard the box and never return.

But there is no such thing as absolute security in life and Little Bit determined to make the most of her time with Big Tom. She was enthralled with his stories of the great beasts he had seen and what they had said. She came to understand what Big Tom had deduced from his travels. She would sometimes take issue with his conclusions but this did not bother Big Tom one bit. In fact he often seemed pleased that she just wouldn't accept what he said and go along with it. He was gratified and proud that she had learned to think for herself. They had many long conversations and Big Tom found that he loved Little Bit; she of course knew before he did but was kind enough to let him discover that fact for himself.

Big Tom knew that eventually he must leave and pursue whatever destiny awaited him above, but for the time being the two were very happy. Their relationship was intimate which we will discover in another chapter.

Oscar and Susan were likewise very happy and planning on pursuing their own destinies. The two would intersect shortly via the medium of Captain Scott.

CHAPTER TWENTY SEVEN

The time came for Big Tom's departure when Little Bit was laden heavy with the next generation that Big Tom hoped would find their own meaning to this life, and it was not without sadness that he withdrew. In fact if Little Bit had not insisted that this was what he said he would and should always do, he might have given in and stayed. But he pushed on and found a nearby box. He was too large to climb in and therefore climbed on top, "aboard" you might say. He clamped a claw on the ascending rope and began to yank it down.

Above on the surface Captain Scott was approaching. Seeing this abnormality, a bouncing buoy on a calm sea he had to investigate.

When the lobster trap broke through the surface the sight of Big Tom on the top of the trap surprised Captain Scott and the whole crew. They were even more surprised when Big Tom clambered up the last length of rope and scuttled out on to the deck. He raised his claw in a motion that reminded Captain Scott of a salute. Captain Scott was immediately charmed. Penny, Captain Scott's daughter we have met before, ordered a large bucket of seawater to be placed beside the wheel where he could keep an eye on his new "mate." The bucket eventually rested beside the ships wheel where Penny and Captain Scott could easily garner the clues that their new crewmember would dispense.

CHAPTER TWENTY EIGHT

So now we have seen how Big Tom, Alberto, Susan and Oscar have all arrived at Alberto's restaurant and Susan and Big Tom's chance meeting on her wedding day.

Big Tom was to see Oscar and Susan throughout the years. Oscar's hair turned a bit gray, and Susan's steps were halting and not quite as swift. Big Tom was surprised that the couple, even Alberto and Captain Scott, who were frequent visitors, seemed to be aging right before his eyes. But Big Tom finally worked it out that although the land was the domain of man, his standing as a lobster gave him an extraordinary life span. At first he saw this as a joke perpetrated on his species, then he had empathy for the humankind that shared this world with him, but finally came to the conclusion that things were the way they were, and he had done the best he could to utilize his life to try and gain some understanding. He wondered if this was enough. But decided that this was the only conclusion he could reach given that he was, to use the metaphor, the defendant, the judge and the jury.

And his life was not without its small rewards and pleasures. Big Tom always looked forward to Oscar and Susan's arrival.

Susan would always come to his tank and speak softly and admiringly to him. Oscar would always tip his head and inquire as to his health. Quite by accident Oscar discovered that his swinging pocket watch, which he was never without, would always excite Big Tom.

Big Tom himself didn't understand why this activity enthralled him, but he always enjoyed it, and Oscar would forever indulge him.

On more than one occasion Alberto, Captain Scott, Susan and Oscar would stand around Big Tom's tank and marvel at his reaction to Oscar's swing watch. "Must be some appointment he is planning," they would all chuckle. They didn't, and couldn't have known how close to the truth they were.

CHAPTER TWENTY NINE

So many years passed in the manner that years have a way of doing. Waiters and waitresses came and went, fashions came and went, car and clothes and those things that seem to give an air of permanence only to be supplanted by the next new and better thing.

We acquire things that seem to make us happy or make our lives easier and believe, even momentarily, that we simply could not live without these accoutrements. But anyone, or by rights of our tale, anything, that has observed and given even the slightest regard to this journey will realize that "things" are merely the debris of life. The thing that gives life value are the people and relationships we have, encounter, develop, endure as well as enjoy and revel within. Hundreds perhaps thousands, tens of thousands of varied items may pass through your life some perhaps without even a brief awareness. It is sad to admit that some of these "items" will be people whom you pass in life and don't notice. You are not alone in this habit, for many of those same people you have slipped past without any recognition have, in fact, slipped past you with no recognition of you.

Everyone is not a friend, and everyone is not your concern, the people that gather, as if they were a family, regardless of any relation, these are the most valuable things we experience in life. This is at once the greatest gift and the most frightful affliction. The old saying goes after some tragedy like a fire, or tornado, "they were just things and things can be replaced." There is often a reason things become "old sayings," cliches if you will. That reason is because their truth is undeniable and self-evident.

The trick of time for young and old people is to accept the moment they find themselves in and believe that this image of permanence is a reflection of permanence. Though delusional it is to feel that what is, "here and now", will always be.

A further delusion is that what is now has always been. The future we cannot know but the past is routinely revised and revamped to rationalize motives personal and universal. This does present those of us living here in this moment with a bit of a problem. We can't live like there is no tomorrow, often, not always, that tomorrow will, and does come.

On that fateful day for which it does not come for us personally little can be said and even less to be known. But, as Big Tom had surmised, the business of living is to live. So the cliché that the only constant thing in the universe is that nothing is constant but its ever-changing nature, is glib and perfectly correct conjecture we can offer.

Still we do resist change. Even if that change is perceived to make our lives better and emotionally, even violently protest that change that diminishes our lives is by definistion, "bad".

And so that storm of emotion came upon Big Tom and, needless to say, Oscar, when Susan came to the end of her journey.

Big Tom had noticed that Oscar and Susan had been missing their usual appearances, but, as time wore on, Oscar did emerge but always alone. When he first began to return to the restaurant he sat in a remote corner and made no contact with Big Tom.

Some times Captain Scott would come and visit for a few moments, and Alberto was always nearby. Alberto seemed to anticipate his old friend's mood and would step to his side at a moment's notice. It was quite sometime later, perhaps a season, Big Tom noticed that the summer months brought many new faces, but these had become less frequent and Oscar assumed a more relaxed posture. Oscar began to nod at Big Tom from across the room. Big Tom would always wave his antenna as a friendly gesture.

Big Tom understood that Susan had died, and, further, that Oscar would naturally be saddened. Big Tom himself was sad and felt that his life was somewhat diminished by her absence. But time, at least in the only way we understand it, moved on. The atmosphere of Alberto's was a comfort for Oscar and little by little he made his way back to Big Tom's tank to inquire how he was getting on. Big Tom would always be very active and tried to comfort Oscar, whom he considered a friend, in any way he could imagine.

Oscar would sometimes get a little teary-eyed when he would take out his pocket watch. When he would swing it back and forth, Big Tom would wave his claws in unison. This always brought a smile back to Oscar's face and that delighted Big Tom to no end.

The weeks slipped into months and then years, and yet this atmosphere was never quite lifted. The world outside Big Bay and to some extent Big Bay itself grew, but Alberto's customers began the slow ebb tide that was to bring the business to the crisis it was facing when Bob had uttered those fateful words, "I'll arrange everything."

As disclosed previously, Bob thought that the extent of his handling the arrangements would be to put up some home printed signs for the event. What he had not counted on was the advent of social media and the frenzy, perhaps it would be more correct to say "firestorm" that would ensue.

The buzz became omnipresent and was destined to attract local and regional media outlets. Such outlets are always starved for content, and no one would pass up a chance to spend a day in the old resort village.

CHAPTER THIRTY

Big Bay was fairly crushed with people. The curious, the inhabitants and, of course those throngs of media. It was said that every person, every building, every bird, every fly, fish, dog and cat that were present on that day were also present on video. The cats of course considered themselves the stars of the show, which they were. To suggest to the local feline residents would be met with total indifference and the expectation of some worthy morsel.

The world watched as the harsh glare of world attention focused on Alberto's and the "drastic actions" they planned to perpetrate on this, not really defenseless creature; Big Tom could have held his own if he could have debated, but being a mere crustacean he was at the mercy of his "exploiters".

There were interviews with Captain Scott and even a highly edited rebroadcast of his prior appearance. Captain Scott only took the precaution of instructing Penny to cover her ears. Captain Scott let loose such a stream of acrimonious language on the reporters that they feared not only for their jobs, but their very lives.

Alberto himself was teary eyed when hammered by a cable news reporter. He was saved somewhat by Bob's suggesting that harsh economic times were more to blame than any desire of his father, or their business, to auction off "Big Larry." It was a sad commentary on the times and the plight of small businesses everywhere. Had this not been a live remote shot there is no doubt that Bob's common sense declaration would have been edited into some twisted form resembling Captain Scott's first appearance. The "news" is less about fact and more about drama. If was often said that the only worthwhile segment was the weather and then reason for that counsel was because the admitted up-front that they were guessing at best and lying at worst.

It was under these acrimonious conditions that, for many, the sad affair began. It started slowly, no one wanting to be the first, but many of the locals wishing the best for Alberto dug deep into their threadbare pockets.

Then in the spirit of competition the bidding became heated. Anyone who has ever witnessed this type of event knows that it takes on a "life of its own." It is somehow in our make-up to want to win at anything and some were swept up in this fever. The character grew to a crescendo and was seemingly drawing to a close when a weak, but clear voice cut through the sputtering crowd.

Alberto who had sat to the side and allowed Bob to run the whole affair rose to his feet. "What was that?" Alberto stepped to Bob's side. From out of the crowd the voice rose again. "I said I would double the last bid."

A murmur ran through the crowd. The last bid had been driven quite high, owing to the fever that had fallen on the crowd. Bob banged a conk-shell, which he had been using as a gavel and called for silence. The crowd did fall silent, and Bob called out to the unseen bidder. "Please step forward and confirm your offer."

The crowd parted, and the figure emerged. It was Oscar. Alberto stepped to his old friend, "Oscar, sir, are you sure you want to do this?" Oscar nodded, and the crowd at first hushed in shocked silence erupted in cheers and applause.

Oscar would receive so many "pats" on the back and have his hand shaken so violently that he was sure he'd need to be hospitalized. "Glad it's you old man!" many of the locals assured Oscar.

The cable news reporter checked her own make-up and had a big puff of powder thumped onto Oscar's face. Oscar was quick to withdraw a handkerchief and try to dispense with what he considered an artifice. It must be remembered here that the auction winner would receive "Big Larry" to be prepared to any stipulation, that is any preparation. It was assumed that the winner would want him fixed in some sort of "tasty" manner. So when the freshly made-up cable news reporter jabbed the microphone into Oscar's face her first question was "How do you want him prepared?" Without blinking Oscar replied, "To go".

CHAPTER THIRTY ONE

For the entire time that Oscar had resided in Big Bay every person who ever met him knew, just knew, he was a humble and quiet man. It seemed that he preferred to put the social focus on Susan, which of course was where his focus was always drawn. He had never been a loud jovial person. Always genial, cheerful and pleasant but never the center of attention and now he was. And he could not conceal his awkwardness, but stepped quickly like a man on a mission, which of course he was.

Oscar had shocked the totality of attendees at Alberto's, and countless more watching, some bidding, online. When he had asked for Big Tom to be prepared "to go," and utter silence had fallen on the crowd. This was just the proverbial "calm before the storm".

The cable newswoman began to sputter and blather randomly, and then the whole place began to roar. Some of the locals were howling with laughter because they understood what was to come. While those outsiders in attendance were either upset that "Big Larry" was going to be consumed, and/or that this was going to happen without their witnessing the event to either be smug or feel morally superior, whatever their personal preference.

You must recall that many people are most concerned about what other people think of them, when it is painfully obvious that most people only concern themselves with thinking about themselves. This turn of events was totally unexpected and forced many in the audience out of their staunchly held preconceived notions.

When the stunned silence gave way to the roar that gave way to a din that Alberto could hear Oscar mouth, or shout in fact, what his plans were. Alberto's face at first revealed total bewilderment, then his open mouth closed, and a broad smile replaced it.

Alberto motioned to Captain Scott and to Bob who stood nearby as puzzled as everyone else. The men huddled in a tight circle. Oscar made his way, not without difficulty, toward the exit. He was subjected to mistreatment by those who were still too confused to understand what was happening, and lauded by those who understood that Oscar had risen to the challenge and had arrived at an expensive, but very satisfying solution.

CHAPTER THIRTY TWO

The whole crowd from Alberto's spilled out into the street. Bob was leading the procession with Big Tom and his tank on a rolling cart. Oscar, Alberto and Captain Scott followed closely behind. The media people were in full panic – scramble mode as the throng made its way toward the docks. Big Tom understood what was going on, but didn't understand all the commotion or where this excursion might lead.

The crowd pushed out to the end of the longest and broadest of the docks. Here Oscar stopped and stared out to the horizon for a moment. The crowd clambered onto boats and pushed far out onto the deck. Captain Scott held up his hands and urged them back. "We'll all end up in the drink!" He shouted and this settled most everyone down.

Everyone accept the media. As a whole they pushed through and elbowed their way to the front. The cable news lady checked her reflection in a small mirror and then thrust her microphone into Oscar's face.

"Just what are you thinking mister –" Oscar quickly turned around cutting the woman off.

Oscar coughed and withdrew his pocket watch. He often did this when he was contemplating something important and this was an important moment for Oscar. An important moment for Big Bay and for assuredly for Big Tom.

When Oscar began to speak it was in a clear strong voice that captivated everyone present. "Many of you knew my late wife. Her name was Susan for those of you who didn't have the pleasure of knowing her." Oscar nodded and a quiet murmur swept through the crowd.

"She was important to a lot of people and her work has helped many of you here. She was a friend to this community and highly thought of. Of course I am biased. I loved her. But that's no secret. Susan had a lot of love in her heart." Oscar glanced down at Big Tom as Big Tom seemed to be nodding in agreement with what was being said.

"That love wasn't for things and places. Susan had a love for all life. All those creatures that are making this journey with us, that share our same uncertain future."

Captain Scott pulled Penny out of the crowd and drew her to his side. Alberto threw an arm over Bob's shoulder. Oscar continued, "that love she shared with us also included this fellow here." Oscar placed his hand on Big Tom's tank. "We happened to have met him for the first time on our wedding day. But she, we, always looked forward to seeing him at Alberto's." Oscar got a bit more emotional. "When she passed I gave some thought to leaving this place. Going somewhere new. Somewhere that the streets, the people, the smells and my friend here", looking down at Big Tom, "wouldn't remind me of my loss." Oscar glanced around at the faces in the crowd. He lingered on Alberto and then Captain Scott. "Then I realized," Oscar continued, "I would just be compounding my loss by losing all of you. I'd have my memories and of course I will always remember my Susan, but I didn't want to give up living and dwell on the past." Oscar pointed to one side, a habit he developed when training new staffers. "I still had some living to do, for whatever reason that might be, and only if it was to be here and do this today."

Oscar bent down over Big Tom's tank. "This fellow has been a good friend to me. He has been a witness to my life and", Oscar looked up at the crowd with a sly smile, "you couldn't ask for a better listener!" A chuckle zipped through the crowd and a smattering of applause broke out.

Oscar drew himself up to his full height and regarded the crowd. "This creature is my friend. Just as you Captain Scott, Alberto and Bob and many of the rest of you. So as a friend I would like to do him a kindness. At least I think it will be a kindness, after all", Oscar glanced down at Penny, "he has known some of us for all our lives." Penny smiled and clung even tighter to her father. "I remember my Susan told me when we first met this magnificent specimen", Oscar stopped himself. "No that's not quite the right word. He's not just an 'example', he is an individual. Susan wondered if we could, 'sit at his knee' as it were, what things we could learn. What things has he seen and what conclusions has he drawn. What does he think about this life and the trek we all must make and are making?”

Oscar looked up and turned to look back at the sea. “I wonder if this is the right thing? I wonder if this is a kindness. Am I forcing him to leave when I determined that it was the wrong course for me? These are not easy questions. But I learned that you are faced with hard decisions in life. If you are wrong you either determine a course of action to make things right, or you accept that you can’t do anything, face it and learn to live with it.” Oscar looked down at Big Tom, “Old friend, I hope this is the right decision. I believe it is. I believe you should live out your days among your friends.”

Oscar grabbed the side of Big Tom’s tank and heaved it over the edge of the dock before anyone, even Captain Scott or Alberto could stop him, though it’s doubtful they would have tried.

The effort was quite a strain for Oscar and his pocket watch slipped out of his pocket. It dangled for the briefest of moments. Long enough for Oscar to realize it would fall into the water and be lost forever. In that moment he thought, “It is only a thing, it is not Susan, it is a very precious thing, but it is not Susan.”

The watch detached and tumbled into the water just as Big Tom was doing something of the same thing. Big Tom’s belly flop was absolutely immense by comparison to the watch, and there is no doubt that it was unsettling for him, but the watch caught his eye and he snagged it.

He pulled it close and flapped his tail. Lobsters can move surprisingly fast when they utilize this method, and in moments Big Tom was far away from the dock. He didn't really know why he felt compelled to race away, but it was a lucky move. The tumult on the dock had proved too great for its structural integrity.

The dock groaned and then buckled tossing all including Oscar, Alberto, Bob, Penny and Captain Scott into the water. A lucky few who had found vantage points on the boats were spared, but most everyone wound up wet.

Surprisingly Captain Scott, Alberto and Oscar were the first to be highly amused by the affair and began to laugh heartily. The laugh was infectious and soon all were chuckling at the absurd spectacle. It was only later as Oscar was pulled to safety that he cast a watering eye out toward the horizon betraying the sadness at the loss of the watch, a touchstone for the memory of Susan.

CHAPTER THIRTY THREE

About the same time that Oscar was feeling sad and looking out to sea, under that surface and perhaps a few hundred yards, or a fewer meters, Big Tom was settling to the seafloor. He likewise cast an eye toward the open sea, but paused and looked back at the murky water that was the harbor floor. He began to scuttle toward the open sea and clamped firmly, but carefully in his claw was the still ticking watch that Oscar had dropped. Big Tom contemplated this strange turn of events. He had never thought he would be returning to his origins. Never thought that any episode of his life would seem circular, if it indeed was, yet here he found himself on a part of his journey that was taking him back to where his beginnings had gone.

"Well," thought Big Tom, "it seems as if I will find the answer to Mr. Wolfe's question in the most obvious way." "I will go home again." Then almost immediately he was struck with an emotion he had never felt before. He couldn't decide if he was just excited, which he clearly was, or fearful, which he clearly was also. Big Tom had lived and learned enough to know that memory is a cheat in many ways. It tends to either focus only on the bad, or the good, or not allow that most of life is a mixture of both of these elements. Big Tom determined that no matter what his feelings about his current situation the fact remained that he was bound to confront it, learn what he could from it and in some way, he didn't know just how, but in some way he must try to understand.

CHAPTER THIRTY FOUR

No matter what apprehension he felt, Big Tom enjoyed the expanse that lay before him. It wasn't that his tank had been small. It had taken up a very generous portion of Alberto's floor space. But here the seafloor was virtually limitless. Big Tom felt almost giddy when the notion came to him. He nearly pranced and skipped along the terrain. He rolled and tumbled and tasted the essential quality of freedom. He had forgotten that the ocean, in fact the world above and below is filled with dangers. Some hidden and some not so hidden. He realized that there was no such thing as absolute security and even in his tank he had faced the possibility of a quick end to his journey, his life.

But it had been many years since he had "frolicked" and so the admittedly mature lobster gave himself over to having a bit of fun. Still he did keep an antenna tuned for any of those dangers, seen, or as best he could, those unseen. He kept the watch clutched to his side initially to keep it safe, then remembering that it attracted predators, to keep it hidden.

It took Big Tom sometime to find his way back to his home. As he neared his destination he began to encounter an unusual number of much younger lobsters, but there were an exceptional number of large lobsters. Though not as large as Big Tom, they were noticeably bigger than their counterparts. But there was more that Big Tom noticed. These large fellows seemed somehow familiar to

Big Tom. Big Tom began to observe that this assemblage was taking notice of him as well. Of course he was used to being "on display" as it were, but these compatriots were taking a long gander at him and conferring among themselves. Then one of their number would speed away and be out of sight in a moment or two.

This was an enigma. Surely these younger lobsters had seen large lobsters in the wild. Big Tom himself had seen examples of his species that were a third again as large as he was now. "What was it," he pondered, "that seemed so familiar?"

After some time and some wrong turns Big Tom began to recognize what he would come to call his home turf. Though in actuality it had been neither his home or his turf, being that it was seafloor after all. His pace quickened as he mounted the last rock pile. He spied a small female resting in the basin he had constructed to Little Bit's specifications "How many years ago could that have been?" he mused as he advanced on her position. She had her back turned to him and seemed to be contemplating something she held.

Just as he was about to make contact he heard a thundering roar approaching. In a moment he was confronted by a herd of the larger lobsters he had been seeing. This group swept in and around the smaller female to challenge him and protect her. Big Tom stumbled back a few steps.

"Wait a second fellows," Big Tom felt that old feeling that he had nearly forgotten, it was fear. "I don't want any trouble! Just coming back to see my beginnings." There was a murmur that ran through the gathering. "Sort of a trip down memory lane. I mean you no harm and will gladly leave you in peace if you will but allow me."

The group seemed stunned for a moment and then began to take a step forward, their voices rising. Then a small, but sharp voice cut through the din. "Hey, let me through!" The group immediately fell silent.

From Big Tom's point of view the crowd parted as he saw the shorter antenna of the small female making her way towards him. He was perplexed and unsure of what was to happen next.

Presently the last of the group parted and a small female lobster emerged. She clasped a broken pair of human glasses and ambled right up to Big Tom. She raised the glasses, she only needed one lens to look through. The effect as observed by Big Tom was that this female lobster's eyes were large and disconcerting. Big Tom gathered himself. "Ma'am it was not my intention to disturb you. But you see…"

The female lobster raced forward. "It _is_ you!" she fairly shouted.

Big Tom was surprised by this sudden embrace and only manages to mutter "Pardon?"

The female lobster pulled back and held up her broken glasses. "Maybe you need these more than I do!" The whole group of lobsters began to snicker.

Big Tom was nonplussed. "What do you mean?"

The little lobster tossed the glasses to Big Tom and he raised them to his eyes. He was shocked. "Little Bit! I never thought I'd see you again!"

Little Bit raises up on her claws. "Same here. Weren't you off on some sort of quest for reason?"

Big Tom nodded and said, "still am as a matter of fact". He lowered the glasses.

"Then how are you, why are you, I mean what are you doing here?"

Big Tom blew out a long stream of bubbles. "Now that is a long story."

Little Bit cuffed Big Tom with her claw. "Not you", she teased him. "You aren't the type for long stories."

Big Tom moderately chuckled. "You do know me well".

Little Bit lowered her voice and moved closer to Big Tom. "Are you home for good?"

Big Tom pushed the glasses back to Little Bit. "I'm afraid I can only stay a little while. I have a task to complete. I didn't choose it, but the obligation is mine nonetheless." Big Tom glanced around the crowd of large lobsters. "It seems as if you have done well for yourself."

"And by myself!" answered Little Bit. Big Tom patted her claw with his.

"That is my biggest regret. I would have loved to have spent my life here with you and maybe not been so driven…"

"To find out" Little Bit finished his thought.

Big Tom nodded. "I'm afraid I did find out."

Little Bit and the crowd pushed forward. "Tell us" she whispered. "Tell us what it all means."

Big Tom looked off into the distance for a moment. "I can't really tell you what it means for you. I found out that life means something different for every creature." Big Tom looked at Little Bit. "I could have found that here with you."

Little Bit tossed a claw in a dismissive manner. "You had to take that path. I don't regret it not…" she paused and the whole crowd joined in as she concluded, "one little bit!"

Big Tom is surprised but still confused. "I could have discovered that life's meaning is to try and be 'good', whatever that might mean and not to hurt anyone, unless they were going to hurt you or yours. You should try and be helpful and support your friends and even try to understand your enemies. You will always find that you will have 'enemies' and organisms that will wish you harm, even death and there will be nothing you can do to change that. So if it is a, 'you or them situation…' Big Tom glanced at the crowd, "It has got to be you. You know your heart and mind. You can't always know theirs."

Big Tom settled down on the seafloor. "And you never know where life will surprise you. It's like me being back here. It was me finding friends and family on the land. There were those that cared for, and about me, and while I must admit that I often thought of you," "Big Tom looked into Little Bit's eyes, "I can't help but think of them as well."

Little Bit nudged Big Tom's side and he revealed Oscar's pocket watch. "Is that something that reminds you of them?"

Big Tom pulled the watch into full view. "In a way", he said. "This was a token of love given by a couple of my friends to each other." Big Tom lowered the watch. "Sad to say that the female passed away, and the couple had no children. Her man was devastated for a long time before he came back and began to live again." Big Tom paused with emotion. "They had no children, as I said, and I think that, much like this watch, I was a memento of the life they had together."

Big Tom brushed Little Bit's antenna. "I had no such tangible object to remember you by. But then I didn't need one. I had my memories, and I can't tell you how many times I thought of our life together here and laughed and, of course, I cried sometimes as well."

A hush had fallen over the crowd. Big Tom seemed to gather himself and tucked the watch back to his side. "Well, tell me about you. What has your life been like?"

Little Bit glanced around at the crowd of mostly male, mostly larger lobsters and smirks. "You know how you said that there are often surprises in life?"

"Of course" Big Tom replied, "that is sometimes the most rewarding thing in life, the unexpected. Of course it can be an unpleasant thing as well, but…"

Little Bit scrambled up on top of a pile of rocks. "This is going to be a surprise for all of you!"

Big Tom and the other lobsters gathered around the pile of rocks at Little Bit's feet. Little Bit swept a claw over the group. "Tommy I want you to meet your children." Big Tom's antennas went straight up. Little Bit continued, "and kids I want you to meet your father." Pandemonium broke free as Big Tom and Little Bit rushed together and, in turn, were rushed by their offspring.

CHAPTER THIRTY FIVE

A few days turned into weeks which, in turn, turned into months. Big Tom and Little Bit stayed together, even though they both knew it was only a temporary situation.

They passed their time with Big Tom telling Little Bit and his descendants about his travels, the wonders he had seen and sharing laughs with Little Bit in which the younger lobsters feigned interest. These were their parents, after all and, though they were mildly interested in the family history, they had their own lives and interests.

This did not go unnoticed by Big Tom or Little Bit. Big Tom reflected, "There is an old saying I heard on land; youth, it is said, is wasted on the young." Little Bit commented that she had heard a sailor say about how a young man at the age of sixteen had thought his father a fool. But by the age of twenty-one he was amazed at how much the old man had learned.

Big Tom chuckled but was more pleased and proud that Little Bit had taken on the challenge of learning that there was more to the world than their rock pile. He was pleased that she had pondered her own journey. He asked her what she thought the future might hold for their children.

Little Bit had been thoughtful for a moment and said, "They have good genes, and I tried to provide the best for them. And, of course, they have, in you, such a fine example. I'm sure they will be well and successful."

Big Tom was quick to say that he didn't know what type of example he had set, but that she had been "exemplary!" Sitting together and looking out over their brood Big Tom realized that this was the way of all things. The ebb and flow of his life, though longer than some, was still governed by the same parameters. He surmised that perhaps he couldn't know it all because he was a part of it and he would not trade the experience of living the life he had lived, only to discover that in doing so, that in the trade, he would have given up the true meaning of it all. The point of living is to live, and this he had done. He further concluded that any creature that had reflected upon their existence would have to have regret. There were just too many choices and too many "unknowns." "Thus and so, or this and that," he had thought. He pulled the pocket watch up to look at it as these thoughts had come to him. Little Bit was observing him.

"You know what you have to do," she had said.

Though he protested, he knew she was right. "I wouldn't give anything for this time we have had, but you are right. There is something, some unfinished business I must see to."

They all gathered around the old lobster trap as Big

Tom mounted it. He turned and looked at them all. "Perhaps I will return. Life is very improbable and strange." With that he tugged on the buoy-line.

At the surface the buoy bobbed up and down and attracted the attention of the newly refurbished Penny Pincher. At the helm was the now grown Penny, having followed her father into the family business and become quite accomplished in her own right. "What the heck?" She had said and had made a beeline toward the bobbing buoy.

A few moments later the crew was hauling the line and lobster "pot" up when it arrived at the surface with Big Tom standing astride.

In a few more moments Penny was on the radio. "Dad", she said excitedly, "you're not going to believe it!" On the console beside Penny Big Tom stood at attention with a claw raised in the "salute" posture.

At a small office beside the docks Captain Scott sat at the radio. "Say again please," Captain Scott said into the microphone.

Penny's voice crackles through the speaker. "You heard me."

Captain Scott pushed his cap back on his head. "Yes ma'am, I heard you." Captain Scott clicked the microphone again and said, "over". Captain Scott reached for his shirt pocket and withdrew a smart-phone. He spoke aloud to himself saying, "This is going to be big!" Captain Scott tried the phone, but the line was busy so he raced out of the door and on to the dock.

Things had changed so radically in Big Bay that Captain Scott had trouble navigating the throngs of tourists and sightseers. There was a line around the side of the building to get into Alberto's. In these days of social media the story of the large lobster, his human companions and the plight that was felt by many small towns and villages up and down the coast and all around the world the story was something that caught people's imaginations.

Big Bay became "the destination" for a wide spectrum of families and travelers. The hotels and restaurants, as well as the other attractions were packed with these folks everyday of the season. Alberto's found itself at the hub of a once again thriving village. Bob had to hire new staff to help him keep up with the books and there were new wait staff training every day. This is why Captain Scott found himself at the back of the line to get into Alberto's.

Captain Scott, finding the news too pressing, pushed through the line saying, "Pardon, pardon, official town business," he passed a young woman wearing a DoBok (a traditional Taekwondo martial arts outfit). Captain Scott was struck by the young woman's beauty, (it is likely that she later struck his face, but that's another story!)

Captain Scott stepped to the podium where Alberto was directing the in-coming diners and well wishing those that departed. Big Tom's tank stood empty to the side with a sign that read, " Reserved for an absent friend." Though no one had suggested the practice, someone, and then nearly everyone, had begun to toss coins into the tank. Alberto collected the coins and donated the money in Susan's and Oscar's name. It was often hard to keep pace with the mounds of coins that piled up, so the donations were substantial.

Captain Scott pulled Alberto to one side and whispered the news. Alberto grabbed Captain Scott and the two men embraced. "This is wonderful news old friend!" exclaimed Alberto, "just wonderful."

Captain Scott pushed his cap back on his head as he said, "I hope Oscar will see it that way." Throwing a thumb over toward Big Tom's old tank, "that was a pretty penny he put up."

Alberto nodded in agreement. "Yes, of course you are right." Alberto suddenly snapped his fingers and said, "We will make equitable!"

The crowd pushed forward and Captain Scott scrambled through the multitude to exit. He had to reach through the customers and pull himself toward the door. Among those that he unknowingly laid a hand on was the young woman in the DoBok. Reacting instinctively she grabbed Captain Scott's arm and wrenched him out of the crowd and tossed him handily onto the dock in front of Alberto's.

Captain Scott was a long-time widower and now with Penny captaining the Penny Pincher he had time, literally, on his hands. He looked up at the young woman and asked, "Would you like to see my boat?" (Again this is a story for another telling.)

Late that evening the Penny Pincher arrived at the dock with the celebrated lobster aboard. Alberto, Bob and Captain Scott were there to greet them. Oddly Oscar was nowhere to be found. Captain Scott produced his smartphone and called, to no avail. "Where has he gotten off to?" He muttered to himself.

Oscar held his phone up and saw that Captain Scott was the caller. But he couldn't answer. Oscar was sitting on a small stage with a number of people all dressed in academic robes.

Oscar slipped the phone back in his pocket as a young woman at the podium introduced him. Oscar made his way to the podium and subconsciously reached for his watch. Not finding it, of course, he brushed his hand along the side of his suit and carefully approached the podium.

Meanwhile at Alberto's the party reached a fever pitch when Big Tom arrived in a large bucket. Penny had brought him in to applause and shouts of "Welcome home!" And, "The hero that saved our town!" Penny had poured Big Tom into his tank and asked after Oscar, but no one knew where he was. There were toasts and many of the townsfolk had pounded Bob on the back congratulating him on having the original idea to save Alberto's. And all were pleased that Big Tom had found his way back to them. The coins rolled into Big Tom's tanks, and he had to dodge many of a generous contributor contribution. He noted that some of the coins were from other countries and places he had traveled. He wondered if they could ever know what he had seen. It didn't matter of course. He was just thrilled to be "home."

The gala roared on into the evening and it was that later "Chris," short for Christina, and Bob's wife showed all that were still present an online video of Oscar.

The video showed the normally reserved Oscar at the podium and he was heard to say, "So I accept this honor in my late wife Susan's name for it was she who made this her cause and our native region is all the better for it. If I have done anything to push this forward it is only because I had great friends and support and chief among them was Susan." The video was wobbly and of poor quality, but everyone wanted to see it over several times.

The crowd sensed that this magical evening was drawing to a close but a few of the old bunch, Captain Scott and his "dangerous" date, Bob and his wife, as well as the staff of Alberto's, including Alberto, were there when Oscar arrived.

A hush fell over all those there as Oscar stepped to Big Tom's tank. There were some who felt, as Captain Scott had indicated, that Oscar might have been "miffed" at having paid so much only to have his philanthropy come to this. But these concerns were quickly dispatched as Oscar approached Big Tom's tank. Oscar reached out his hand and touched the front of the tank. "It is so good to see you old friend! I've," Oscar glanced around the room, "we have missed you."

Big Tom scrambled up onto the top of the mound of coins and pulled the watch into view. He raised it above the surface of the tank, and everyone could see it. Oscar exclaimed, "My watch! How did you … where, what…" Oscar stammered as he took the watch from Big Tom.

Oscar gazed into the heart of Big Tom and knew that no matter the fact that they were of such different heterogeneity Big Tom had understood and shared his love for Susan.

EPILOG:

Though Big Tom was a lobster, and they can live long and protracted lives, he, like Oscar, Alberto and Captain Scott had lived the vast majority of that life. In recognition of that fact Big Tom was "retired" to the, "Native Wildlife Preserve," the facility that Oscar had funded and which was dedicated in Susan's name.

There he lived out the rest of his days and was frequently visited by the whole gang. He did make some "outings" though. He was a guest at Captain Scott's wedding, as well as Bob and Chris' ceremony. The staff at the large tank preserve had constructed a "travel tank" for Big Tom. He enjoyed these visitations, he was always glad to go anywhere, but in later years he was equally as glad to get home.

There was some discussion among the staff, as well as Alberto, Oscar and Captain Scott, some of it heated, addressing the idea that perhaps Big Tom should be returned to the sea, but it was finally concluded that his life had largely been spent with them as their lives had largely been spent with him. Therefore he should live out his days in the comfort and safety within the preserve. In the end it gave them all comfort.

The town of Big Bay had received such an economic jolt it became the favorite destination of many tourist and curious travelers and remains so even to this day.

Penny expanded her father's business and was very successful. She did note that there was an extraordinary increase in the number of larger lobsters in the catch. It became her practice, and indeed is the practice industry wide now that large lobsters are never kept for harvest, but returned to the sea. This practice is generally held to be good for the species, and it surely seems to be.

This fact seemed to please Oscar and he knew in his heart that Susan would be pleased as well.

THE END

Big Tom
wishes you
fair weather
and calm
waters as
you start
your own
journey.

9 781963 295757